6/16

Case of Foul Play on a School Day

By J.L. Anderson

Illustrated by David Ouro

Rourke
Educational Media
rourkeeducationalmedia.com

www.rourkeeducationalmedia.com

Edited by: Keli Sipperley
Cover layout by: Tara Raymo
Interior layout by: Jen Thomas
Cover and Interior Illustrations by: David Ouro

Library of Congress PCN Data

Case of Foul Play on a School Day / J.L. Anderson
(Rourke's Mystery Chapter Books)
ISBN (hard cover)(alk. paper) 978-1-63430-386-6
ISBN (soft cover) 978-1-63430-486-3
ISBN (e-Book) 978-1-63430-581-5
Library of Congress Control Number: 2015933742

Printed in the United States of America,
North Mankato, Minnesota

Dear Parents and Teachers:

With twists and turns and red herrings, readers will enjoy the challenge of Rourke's Mystery Chapter Books. This series set at Watson Elementary School builds a cast of characters that readers quickly feel connected to. Embedded in each mystery are experiences that readers encounter at home or school. Topics of friendship, family, and growing up are featured within each book.

Mysteries open many doors for young readers and turn them into lifelong readers because they can't wait to find out what happens next. Readers build comprehension strategies by searching out clues through close reading in order to solve the mystery.

This genre spreads across many areas of study including history, science, and math. Exploring these topics through mysteries is a great way to engage readers in another area of interest. Reading mysteries relies on looking for patterns and decoding clues that help in learning math skills.

Whether readers are reading the books independently or you are reading with them, engaging with them after they have read the book is still important. We've included several activities at the end of each book to make this both fun and educational.

Do you think you and your reader have what it takes to be a detective? Can you solve the mystery? Will you accept the challenge?

Rourke Educational Media

Table of Contents

Chapter
One

The Empty Box

Queeneka liked to imagine that she was a queen sometimes. She even practiced a queenly wave and worked on her posture in front of her bedroom mirror. Queen of what country, she didn't know, but she at least felt like royalty at Watson Elementary School. She was one of the most popular students in third grade and kids often came to her to help solve their problems and mysteries.

She wanted to be an actress someday and star in a TV show called *Queen of Fashion*. And speaking of fashion, when Queeneka stepped on the bus that day, she was pleased to see that Bus Driver McCool had on a pair of jeans that weren't so ripped at the knees. The bus driver seemed to be cleaning up nicely after he asked Coach Shorts to marry him.

Queeneka watched as a set of parents waited with their kid at the next bus stop. The parents hugged

the wild-haired girl before she stepped on the bus. The girl's name was Keely, and talk about a fashion nightmare! Keely immediately shoved a stained peach, polka-dotted sweatshirt over a fluorescent yellow T-shirt with a bold logo on the front.

She thought the logo looked like a dog, but she couldn't get a good enough look and she didn't want to make any assumptions. She loved mysteries and knew a good detective shouldn't make any guesses until there was enough evidence.

"Ruff ruff!" Klaude called out to Keely. He was funny. Queeneka could imagine him starring in a comedy TV show someday. Maybe the two of them would be on the same TV station. They'd bring Watson Elementary School lots of fame.

Keely stared Klaude down. "Are you calling me a dog? That's not nice, you know," she said.

Queeneka watched as Klaude shrank in the bus seat. "No—sorry. You know I like to joke around. I wasn't trying to be mean, promise. I was barking because of your dog shirt," Klaude said.

A girl named Divya and her shy friend who liked to draw, Javier, looked over to see what was going on. They looked confused. It didn't help that Keely's dog shirt was now covered up by the ugly sweatshirt.

Keely's face broke out in red spots that looked like giant freckles only a lot less dark. "My parents started a business and they've gone a bit crazy buying stuff with their logo on it. They've even started sending stuff to school."

Her parents were sending their business things to school? Queeneka wondered what exactly they'd sent. If her parents were going to give each student a shirt like Keely's, Queeneka hoped the color would be teal instead of florescent yellow. Teal really made her brown eyes pop.

Keely had to be a size or two smaller than Queeneka. Queeneka made a mental note to go through her closet to find a fashionable sweater she'd outgrown to bring Keely the next day.

Queeneka chatted with Veronica and her friends for the rest of the bus ride. Everyone talked about what they thought Bus Driver McCool and Coach Shorts' wedding would be like. Queeneka imagined the tall coach wearing a white track suit holding a basketball as she walked down the aisle. Or maybe her bouquet would be a collection of tennis balls, baseballs, and ping pong balls glued together.

That would be much worse than a fluorescent yellow shirt with a dog business logo on it! Queeneka planned on slipping some fashion advice to Coach Shorts. She didn't know much about wedding styles, but she really loved dresses.

After Bus Driver McCool parked the bus, Keely ran off. She headed in the direction of the cafeteria. Or maybe the gymnasium. *Keely can sure run fast*, Queeneka thought.

"I think you really hurt her feelings, Klaude," Queeneka said.

Divya stuck up for Klaude, which kind of surprised

Queeneka. Divya always seemed to be annoyed by Klaude. "I don't think he meant to," Divya said.

Queeneka let it go. She had more important things to worry about—like how she planned to pull her long braids back into a ponytail for PE class.

******

Coach Shorts wore long, black-and-white striped track pants and a black shirt with the school mascot on it—a smart looking white owl wearing a pair of glasses. Queeneka had never seen Coach Shorts smile so much.

"Keely's parents donated a set of three kickballs to the physical education department," Coach Shorts said. "To celebrate, let's have a free play day!"

The class cheered. But when Coach Shorts went to pass out the kickballs, the box was empty.

The Search Starts

Everyone gasped.

Keely ducked her head down as everyone turned to stare at her. Her face was freckly-red again. Poor girl, Queeneka thought. She still had on the ugly sweatshirt over the florescent yellow shirt.

"Where are they?" Coach Shorts asked.

Nobody answered her.

"Does this mean that we can't have a free play day?" Klaude asked.

"Get to playing, just don't go past the line of hedges where I can't see you," Coach Shorts said. She hunted all over the gymnasium and went into the PE supply closet to search for the missing kickballs. Several students helped her, including Queeneka. The gym opened up to an outdoor courtyard where some kids jumped ropes or hula hooped. Another group of kids walked around the gym's outdoor track

near the hedges, chatting away like a mystery wasn't unfolding in front of their very eyes.

Keely stood off to the side by the basketball goal, kicking a small beanbag up into the air.

"A delivery woman dropped off the kickballs late yesterday afternoon. I don't know where they could've gone," Coach Shorts said.

"I bet a kickball thief got 'em!" Klaude yelled in a fake Southern accent. Some kids laughed.

Klaude could be right. It was possible the kickballs had been stolen.

"Did you see the kickballs in the gym this morning?" Queeneka asked, using her queenliest of voices. She thought it made her sound more like a detective. Plus, Klaude had started a trend of talking in a different voice.

Veronica laughed like Queeneka was telling a joke.

Coach Shorts took a deep breath before speaking. "The box was here this morning and I assumed the kickballs were still inside. The last time I saw them was when I opened the box after the delivery woman dropped the package off."

Queeneka needed more information if she was going to help solve the case of the missing kickballs.

"What did they look like?" she asked.

Keely stopped kicking the beanbag and moved closer to the group of volunteers.

"The kickballs were red with a bright yellow design of a dog—" Coach Shorts started to say, but Keely cut her off.

"It's the logo for my parents' new business," Keely said. That's all the information she gave.

Queeneka had to dig a little deeper. "Tell us more about your parents' new business," she said, still using her queenly voice. It made her feel like a TV talk show host as well as a detective.

"Yeah. What is the business about?" Veronica asked in what Queeneka thought was a British accent. It wasn't such a good accent, if you asked her. Besides, Queeneka had asked the question first.

The volunteers huddled in together to find out more information.

Keely paused. "Well...they're looking after dogs."

"Like a doggy day care?" Divya asked.

"It's different," Keely said, but she didn't explain how.

"I have an idea!" Queeneka said. She liked the way everyone turned their attention back to her.

"We should inspect the box to see if there are any clues," she said, so excited that she forgot to use her queen voice.

"Good idea," said Coach Shorts. She pulled out the box in the center of the gymnasium for the volunteers to inspect.

It looked just like a typical brown cardboard box. It was slightly rippled as if it had gotten damp and then dried. That didn't give Queeneka much information. She sort of expected to see it covered with greasy handprints or some other type of evidence that would lead the group straight to the kickball thief–or thieves.

"I'm sure the kickballs will show up," Divya said. She and Javier walked off to play a game of tetherball. Several of the other volunteers wandered off to enjoy the free time play too now that the mystery didn't seem to be going anywhere.

Not Queeneka, though. She was determined to recover the lost kickballs. Veronica stayed right by her side to help.

Chapter
Three

Queeneka Gathers Clues

Keely looked over at Queeneka as she turned the box every which way to see if there was a clue she'd missed. Veronica lost interest in the cardboard box pretty quickly.

Just as Queeneka was about to lose interest in the box, too, a small sheet of paper labeled Invoice slipped out of a cardboard flap.

The ink on the invoice was blurred from getting damp, but Queeneka could see that it came from a sports company. No surprise there, she thought.

There was a sample of the logo that was printed on the kickballs, but the ink had washed out. If Queeneka squinted, she thought that maybe it was a drawing of a dog sitting down, perhaps in a field of grass. There were some words in quotes underneath the dog drawing.

Ugh! If only the box hadn't gotten wet, then she'd be able to read the entire business slogan. As it was, she could only understand some of the words: "making dog" and "varnish" or "vanish."

"Varnish" didn't make sense. Wasn't that the kind of smelly stuff her father put on their wood floor at home? Considering how shiny the wood floor was in the gymnasium, there surely had to be some kind of varnish on it.

The word "vanish" didn't make much sense either. What kind of company would make dogs vanish?

Queeneka knew there had to be dog thieves out there, but who in their right mind would build a business around stealing dogs?

"This doesn't make sense," Veronica said.

"You're absolutely right," Queeneka said.

If Queeneka had to squint much more to read the words, she'd get a few wrinkles like the school principal, Mrs. Holmes. Not that wrinkles were bad. No, not at all. She thought the principal was pretty and fashionable, actually. It was just that Queeneka had a famous future ahead of her and she was way too young for wrinkles.

When Queeneka looked up, Keely was standing

right next to her and Veronica. This was a good time to start asking some questions and getting some answers. Queeneka wanted to hurry up and find the kickballs so she could play a fun game with her friends before PE ended.

"Have any other items with your parents' business logo disappeared?" Queeneka asked.

Keely shook her head. "No. The only other thing my parents sent to the school was a bunch of postcards for the teachers along with some chocolates. The teachers all got the postcards as far as I know."

Queeneka sighed. There went that teal shirt she dreamed up earlier. Not like she had much room in her closet anyway. She really did need to clean out some clothes.

Ack! She was getting sidetracked.

"Why do you think the kickballs disappeared?" Veronica asked.

Ooh, that was a good question, Queeneka thought.

Keely shrugged. "Who would've wanted those kickballs?"

That was another good question. Queeneka needed to figure out who had the motivation to steal the kickballs. They clearly weren't lost because Coach

Shorts and the volunteers would've found them by now.

The only place they hadn't checked was Coach Shorts' office. Maybe someone moved them there by accident. But without the box? It didn't make much sense but it was worth checking.

How would Queeneka search the office without making it seem that Coach Shorts had done something with the kickballs?

Queeneka had her chance when someone yelled out in pain moments later. Coach Shorts rushed out to the courtyard area to check on the noise. Almost everyone in the class followed her. Even Veronica left Queeneka's side to see what was going on. Only Keely remained.

Queeneka was dying to find who cried out and why, but with Coach Shorts busy, this was her chance to give the office a quick search.

"What are you doing?" Keely asked as Queeneka sneaked into Coach Shorts' office.

"Looking for clues, duh," Queeneka said. She nearly whooped a cheer when she saw something exciting sitting on Coach Shorts' desk.

Chapter Four

Getting Closer!

"What's so exciting?" Keely asked. "The kickballs aren't in here, are they?"

Queeneka couldn't expect Keely to understand, but she pointed to a copy of a bridal magazine lying on Coach Shorts' desk. The magazine cover photo was a tall woman who sort of looked like the coach, only not as muscular. She wore a beautiful white gown with everything Queeneka loved about fancy dresses: sparkles, frills, and lace.

"Maybe Coach Shorts doesn't plan on wearing a white track suit when she says 'I do' to Bus Driver McCool," Queeneka said.

Keely laughed. It was a real laugh, not fake like Veronica's laugh could sometimes be. Queeneka told her how she'd pictured the ball-themed bouquet. Keely laughed again. Keely's hair might've been wild, and Queeneka would've never picked out her clothes, but she was really nice and she had a great laugh.

"We better get out of here before we get caught," Queeneka said.

"Do you think everything is okay?" Keely pointed to the crowd of students gathered around a kid sitting on the ground in the courtyard.

"I sure hope so," Queeneka said. She walked over with Keely to find out what was going on, deep in thought.

This was a most unusual PE day. Most of the time, Coach Shorts had them all sweating by working out at stations and then running laps. They didn't get free play days very often and it was rare that they got new PE equipment. Not like they got to actually use the kickballs since they were missing.

Queeneka hoped to fix that soon! If it didn't work out with the TV fashion show thing, she dreamed of being a detective. She really liked helping people, though she was having trouble helping to find the missing stuff Keely's parents had sent the school.

When Queeneka got closer, she saw Javier was the kid on the ground. Turns out, Divya had spiked the tetherball for the win in a game against Javier. She must've hit the ball hard because it bopped Javier in the nose and he started bleeding.

Nurse Strongman was already there with a first aid kit and an ice pack. "I don't think anything is broken. The ball must have hit you in the right spot to bleed so much. Or should I say wrong spot?" Nurse Strongman said.

"I'm okay," Javier said. He wasn't trying to talk in an accent but his voice sounded different because his nose was all plugged up.

"I'm so sorry!" Divya said, repeating it over and over again.

"I'm okay," Javier repeated. "That was the best winning hit I've ever seen."

Several people laughed, including Keely. Divya didn't even crack a smile.

Coach Shorts blew a whistle. "Back to order! We have fifteen minutes of free time play remaining. Get back to playing!"

Queeneka used this time to adjust the braids in her ponytail and to think through the kickball case. She hadn't found a suspect and she couldn't be certain the kickballs were stolen. That was the most likely explanation so far since no one had found a trace of them.

Queeneka walked some laps around the indoor track and Keely joined her. Both of them seemed lost in thought.

When the custodian came in to clean up the tetherball area after the Divya/Javier accident, Queeneka had an idea. Perhaps the custodian knew something about the kickballs. After all, the custodian had likely cleaned the gymnasium at the end of the school day. The kickball package had already been delivered by then.

"Hi," Queeneka said to the custodian in her queenly voice.

The custodian smiled and said, "Hi."

"Did you happen to see a large, damp cardboard box yesterday?" Queeneka asked.

There was a long pause and Queeneka wondered if the custodian had even heard her question. She had just started to repeat it when the custodian said, "You know, I did! When I cleaned the gym last night, I saw a box near the basketball hoop."

Finally, Queeneka might get some solid clues! Keely didn't say a thing, though her skin had turned reddish again. "Did you happen to see what was inside the box?" Queeneka asked.

"Red balls with yellow writing," the custodian said. "I wasn't being nosy. Promise. I needed to know if the box was full of trash or not."

"So you didn't trash the kickballs?" Queeneka asked.

The custodian gave her a stern look that could've rivaled the look the school principal, Mrs. Holmes, gave to troublemakers at Watson Elementary School. "I would never throw away something important!"

"I didn't think so, not for a minute," Queeneka said. "Sorry if I sounded rude. The kickballs are missing and I'm trying to help find them."

The custodian relaxed. "I see. Sorry I don't have more information."

Well, this was interesting! The custodian had confirmed that the kickballs were still there after getting delivered in the afternoon. The custodian locked up after cleaning, so that meant the kickballs had gone missing this morning. Queeneka felt like she was getting somewhere.

Chapter
Five

New Suspect

Queeneka spent the remaining time in PE walking laps with Keely and Veronica. They talked about Javier's nose and if he would get a black eye. Divya would feel really awful about that, they all agreed.

Queeneka didn't find the kickballs before the end of the class. "I hope I can find the kickballs before we have PE again. Maybe Coach Shorts will give us another free time play if I do."

"Maybe! Coach Shorts has really been in a good mood," Veronica said.

After PE, it was time to visit the library. Queeneka always loved going to the library to read nonfiction books about fashion or fiction mystery stories. As she collected the books she needed to return, she saw some chopsticks and paint supplies in her teacher's work corner. Mr. Hambrick liked to call it the "construction zone." More importantly, Queeneka saw something round and red with a big splash of yellow that looked very suspicious.

Keely and Veronica didn't seem to notice, and Queeneka didn't want to draw their attention to it. She wanted to interview Mr. Hambrick alone.

"I'll catch up with you girls in the library soon. I need to talk to Mr. Hambrick about something important," Queeneka said to Veronica and Keely. On TV shows, people talked more when they chatted with the host one-on-one.

"Hi, Mr. Hambrick," Queeneka said once the other students headed off to the library. Queeneka didn't want to miss story time, but hopefully she'd solve the case immediately, a true PE hero.

"What can I help you with, Queeneka?" Mr. Hambrick asked. His beard was so thick that Queeneka couldn't tell if his mouth had even moved.

"Uh—" Queeneka suddenly wasn't sure how to start her interrogation. She looked away from Mr. Hambrick's beard and thought about running off to the library. The new planet posters hanging on the wall and bright pictures of the solar system caught her attention.

"Didn't there used to be another planet?"

Queeneka asked.

Mr. Hambrick's eyebrows were bushy like his beard, and they lifted up like he wasn't expecting that question. "Yes, you're right. It was called Pluto. Here, I'll show you something."

BINGO! Mr. Hambrick led Queeneka right into the construction zone to show her a model of the solar system he was building. Mr. Hambrick was a good teacher and always had the best displays. He'd even won Watson Elementary Teacher of the Year.

Mr. Hambrick pointed at several foam balls as he named the planets. He talked about the way they orbited around the sun, which happened to be the suspicious red ball that he was in the process of painting yellow. "This is where Pluto hangs out," Mr. Hambrick said, pointing to an imaginary blank space. "It used to be the ninth planet, but now scientists call it a dwarf planet instead."

Mr. Hambrick listed off a couple of other facts about the planets that Queeneka found interesting, but she needed to get to the bottom of the case as quickly as possible. She also didn't want to miss anymore story time.

"Where did you find such a cool model for the sun?" Queeneka asked. She used her queen accent so she wouldn't lose confidence.

Mr. Hambrick's bushy eyebrows scrunched down. "Why do you ask?"

Was that guilt in his voice? Queeneka thought.

"It's just that we were missing three kickballs in PE this morning and this one sort of fits the description," Queeneka said. "Did it have a logo on it before you started painting?

Mr. Hambrick crossed his arms over his chest.

Between the way he was standing, his beard, and his red flannel shirt, Queeneka thought he looked like a lumberjack. An upset lumberjack!

"Not that any student should have to worry about it, but teachers have been having budget issues. I have to be extra creative these days to save money," Mr. Hambrick said. "You better hurry or you're going to miss library time. You'll be learning a whole lot more about the planets when you get back."

"Thanks for your help," Queeneka said.

As she walked off, she replayed their conversation. Yes, that did seem like guilt in his voice. And his comment about the budget and being creative made him sound extra guilty. Queeneka had a lead suspect in the case.

Guilty Teacher?

Queeneka was so lost in thought that she bumped into the school secretary, Mr. Sleuth, in the hallway outside of the library. He must've been on his way back to the library. Mr. Sleuth was so beanpole tall that she wasn't sure how she could've missed him!

"Instead of hall passes, we might need to issue licenses to walk in the hallway," Mr. Sleuth said.

Queeneka stopped walking to try to understand what he meant.

"It's a joke, Ms. Queen," Mr. Sleuth said.

She liked it when he called her that. It was part of the reason she felt like royalty at Watson Elementary School.

"Oh," Queeneka said. "Can I ask you something?"

Mr. Sleuth laughed. "You just did."

"Fine. Can I ask you something else?" Queeneka said.

"You just did again!" Mr. Sleuth said.

Queeneka wasn't getting the school secretary's jokes at all today. "Never mind," she said, and was just about to head into the library when Mr. Sleuth apologized.

"Sorry, Ms. Queen. What is your concern?" Mr. Sleuth asked.

"What are some ways that teachers have to be creative because of the budget issues?" Queeneka asked.

The smile wiped off of Mr. Sleuth's face. "I wasn't expecting that sort of question. Well, the teachers here sometimes use their own money to buy things and we often have things donated to us by students' parents—"

"Like Keely's parents," Queeneka said. Now was a good time to confirm if any of the postcards or the chocolates had gone missing or if it was just the kickballs. If anyone would know for sure, it would be Mr. Sleuth since he seemed to know a lot about the things that happened at school.

"Yes, like Keely's parents. I heard they made a donation to Coach Shorts," Mr. Sleuth said.

So Mr. Sleuth hadn't heard the kickballs had

gone missing yet. Queeneka didn't fill him in on that detail, but she asked him about the postcards and chocolates.

Mr. Sleuth told her that he watched the teachers pick up the postcards with his very own eyes. "Many of the teachers ate the chocolates before they left the office," he said. "In fact, I had to clean up some wrappers myself! Only one teacher shared any of their chocolates with me. That would be your teacher, Mr. Hambrick. He must've felt bad because I caught him taking paper from the copy machine for one of his class projects. See? That's one way that teachers are being creative with less money to spend these days."

Hmm. So Mr. Hambrick had been taking paper from the copy machine? Could that even be considered stealing? Queeneka didn't have an answer for that, but it did seem to count as being sneaky.

She felt even more certain that Mr. Hambrick took the kickballs, at least one of them. Imagine, a Teacher of the Year award winner stealing from the PE department!

"Thanks for talking to me," Queeneka said to Mr. Sleuth. "And sorry for bumping into you." She waited for him to make an awful joke, but he didn't.

"No problem, Ms. Queen. I'm in the office if you need anything else."

The person Queeneka needed to talk to in the office was Mrs. Holmes. The principal of Watson Elementary School would certainly want to find out if one of the teachers was a thief.

Queeneka decided to wait to talk to Mrs. Holmes until she could search her homeroom to see if she could find the remaining two missing kickballs or any other clues.

******

"Is everything all right?" Veronica asked when Queeneka joined the class in the library. Keely was sitting close to her.

The librarian was reading them a chapter from a Hardy Boys mystery book. Queeneka had missed the beginning part of the story and could hardly pay attention. She wanted to be as good at solving crimes as the Hardy Boys were.

"Mr. Hambrick might've stolen one of the kickballs," Queeneka whispered.

"I doubt it," Keely said and ran her hands through her wild hair. Her fingers got stuck and she tugged out a knot. "Just let it go. Who cares about the kickballs anyway?"

Why didn't Keely care more? Queeneka wished she could've just let the case go, but she felt it was her duty to find out, even if she wouldn't like the answer.

Chapter Seven

Queeneka's Quest for More Clues

Queeneka searched around the classroom for the missing balls later that morning. She looked in the supply closet but the only thing suspicious was a stack of plain white paper—probably what Mr. Sleuth had caught her teacher taking red-handed.

Where was Mr. Hambrick hiding the other two kickballs, if he had them at all?

Mr. Hambrick's desk was covered with paper and lots of other stuff. There was hardly any room for him to hide such a large object. At least he had a beautiful window view of the outdoor playground by the gym. A group of fourth graders played outside now. They ran around wild, which made Queeneka think Coach Shorts gave them free play time, too.

"It's time to get back to work, Queeneka," Mr.

Hambrick said.

"Yeah, or he's going to send you on a one way trip to see Mrs. Holmes!" Klaude said.

Queeneka rolled her eyes at Klaude and went back to doing some research. Only she couldn't focus on the solar system and the way the planets orbited the sun. Queeneka wanted to check the cubby area where students stored their things. She pretended she was looking for a pencil.

She might've just imagined it, but Mr. Hambrick gave her that stern lumberjack stare. If her teacher shaved his beard, he'd look much more stylish. Plus, it would be easier to see his mouth move when he talked. But Queeneka would never be brave enough to tell him that!

The cubby area overflowed with backpacks and jackets. Queeneka moved a sweatshirt out of the way to pat down someone's large backpack. It was puffed up with air, not a kickball. Nothing else seemed bloated enough to be hiding a kickball.

The sweatshirt gave Queeneka an idea, though.

Keely still was wearing her stained peach-polka-dotted sweatshirt. If Queeneka knew what the logo looked like, she would have an even better idea of what she was searching for. Why hadn't she thought of that earlier?

Queeneka was just about to ask Keely if she could check out the logo on her florescent yellow shirt but squeals outside of the window distracted her.

"Those fourth graders are sure having fun," Veronica said.

She was right. Queeneka stared out of the window as one of the fourth grade kids kicked a ball to her friend in the courtyard.

Wait! The ball was red with a blur of yellow. That's all Queeneka could see from the classroom window. She had to get outside to find out if this was one of the two other missing kickballs.

"Mr. Hambrick," she said in her queenliest of voices, "I forgot something in PE this morning. May I go get it, please?"

The classroom's phone line rang, but before Mr. Hambrick answered it, he said, "Go and come right back, Queeneka."

Good thing for that phone call, Queeneka thought. He probably would've never let her go otherwise.

"What are you doing?" Veronica asked.

"I'll explain later," Queeneka said.

Veronica pouted. Queeneka didn't have time to worry about her friend's feelings. Not when Mr. Hambrick might change his mind before he got off the phone.

Queeneka charged out of the room and down the hall to the gymnasium.

Queeneka heard footsteps following her. She ducked behind a bulletin board tree display to find out who it was.

She couldn't believe it!

"Keely? What are you doing?" Queeneka asked.

Keely jumped back when Queeneka stepped out from behind the bulletin board. "You scared me half to death!"

That didn't answer her question. "Did you see the ball, too? Do you think it's the one your parents sent?"

Keely nodded. "We should just let it go," she said. "Those fourth graders can be mean."

No way was Queeneka going to let it go, even if the older fourth graders were mean! She was way too close to solving the case.

Kickball Discovery!

Queeneka forced herself not to look toward Mr. Hambrick's class window. Just imagining his lumberjack stare made her feel less confident as she came near the fourth graders playing kickball.

Now that she was closer on the field, she could see that the ball looked new. One of the biggest kids in fourth grade—and maybe in all of Watson Elementary School—kicked the ball so hard that it flew across the field and landed near Queeneka.

Before the fourth graders could come and get the ball, she bent down and grabbed it. She was turning the ball to see if it had a logo printed on it when Keely stole the ball from her!

"What are you doing?" Queeneka asked.

"I'm going to bring it back to Coach Shorts," Keely

said. "It's evidence."

Sure, Keely's parents had donated the PE equipment, but Queeneka had come to think of this case as hers. "We can't be sure of that until we check—"

"What do you think you're doing, pipsqueaks?" the large fourth grader asked. Her muscles had to make Coach Shorts proud. *She has a future modeling gym clothes*, Queeneka thought.

Queeneka sure didn't want to get into a fight with this kid. Keely swallowed hard. Her face not only looked freckly red, it looked fiery red.

"Nothing to say, huh?" the fourth grader said. "Then give me my ball back!" The fourth grader reached for it. Queeneka thought Keely was a goner.

Keely stood her ground. "It's mine!"

The fourth grader reached over and snatched it from Keely's arms.

"Finders keepers," she said.

Keely looked as though she might tackle her, but before she had a chance, Coach Shorts came over.

"What's going on, girls? And what are you two doing back in PE?" Coach Shorts asked, looking at Queeneka and Keely.

"We're in the process of solving the case of the missing kickballs." Queeneka pointed to the fourth grader. "And I think we found a new lead suspect!"

"Suspect? You're nuts," the fourth grader said. "I'm no thief. I found this ball fair and square near the hedges when I was running laps."

Who would run laps during free time play? Even more important, what was the ball doing near the hedges? Several of the other fourth graders backed her up. There went that lead. Why did this case have to be so complicated?

Coach Shorts grabbed the ball. "I'll take this for now. Thanks for being so concerned about school property, but you two must get back to class or else."

Queeneka certainly didn't want to find out what 'or else' meant, but she was too close to give up now. She started walking back to the main hallway slowly, waiting for Coach Shorts to leave. The fourth graders stuck out their tongues at Keely and Queeneka, then moved on to play a game of foursquare instead.

Queeneka sneaked off toward the hedges on the far side of the outdoor track.

Keely trailed her like a hound. "What in the world are you doing?"

Queeneka ran so fast that her braids seemed to fly in the air. She was too out of breath to explain that if the fourth grader found one of the balls over here, there was a good chance the third and final kickball might be close by.

Queeneka reached the hedges and dropped to her knees to make it easier to search the ground. It didn't take long for her to find her reward—a red ball with a bright yellow dog on it.

But before she could pick it up, Keely kicked it out of the way.

Chapter
Nine

A Twist
in the Case

"What in the world are YOU doing?" Queeneka yelled at Keely. "You're tampering with evidence."

"Will you just please, please let the case go?" Keely asked.

"No way!" Queeneka lunged for the ball.

Just as Queeneka's fingers grazed the ball, Keely pulled her arm back. "I don't want anyone to have the kickballs! It's bad enough that so many of the fourth graders have already seen one of them," Keely said.

It took a moment for this comment to sink in. Queeneka reviewed what she'd learned so far.

Coach Shorts hadn't lost the balls.

The custodian hadn't accidentally thrown them away.

Mr. Hambrick had one of the kickballs. He seemed

guilty but that didn't mean he'd stolen anything. Maybe he had found it just like that huge fourth grader.

Queeneka thought it was strange how Keely hid her shirt with her parents' business logo. She hadn't shared much about the business at all. She'd been following Queeneka's every move about the case and wanted her to quit.

"Where did you go once you got off the school bus?" Queeneka asked. It was an important question, but she ditched the queen accent.

Keely scrunched up her very red face. "Why does it matter?"

"Because I don't think someone stole the kickballs—I think you hid them to begin with!"

Queeneka expected Keely to deny it. Only she didn't.

"You think I don't have any style, and compared to you, I don't have very much. But do you blame me for not wanting to wear this?" Keely peeled off her ugly sweatshirt.

Queeneka finally got a good look at the logo on the florescent yellow shirt. A silhouette of a dog was bent over like it was about to do its business on a patch of

grass! There was a small trash bag off to the side.

The words "making dogs" and "vanish" now made sense. The family's business was called **THE SCOOP TROOP**. Their slogan: "Committed to Making Dog Doo Vanish."

Queeneka didn't know what to say for a moment. That was a pretty rare thing. There's no way she would've worn the shirt. Ever! Even if it was teal.

"Their business is so embarrassing! It was bad enough my parents sent postcards and chocolates to the teachers, but they took it too far by making me wear this shirt and then sending The Scoop Troop kickballs to PE. I ran off the bus this morning, found the kickballs, and then hid them in the hedges while Coach Shorts was busy looking at wedding magazines.

"I'm glad my parents are proud of their business, and I'm proud of them. The thing is that I'm already having trouble fitting in and I don't want to be the dog bottom of everyone's jokes."

Queeneka laughed so hard she snorted. "You are so funny!"

Keely laughed too.

"I planned to pick out a sweater for you to borrow, but maybe you can come over to my house to look through my closet with me," Queeneka said.

Keely smiled. "Sure."

"Should we leave this kickball out here?" Queeneka asked.

Keely shook her head. "No, let's return it to Coach Shorts. My parents wanted the kids to have fun while promoting their business. I need to accept it. The fourth graders found one, so all of Watson will know about it before the final bell rings anyway. The jokes will hopefully wear out."

For Keely's sake, Queeneka sure hoped so.

"You did a good job figuring things out. Thanks for being understanding," Keely said.

******

Yes, Queeneka liked to think of herself as royalty at Watson Elementary School and she loved the way word spread around school how she solved the case of the missing kickballs. Keely had kind of become famous, too, just not in the way she had ever imagined.

Coach Shorts' good mood continued and she let Queeneka's class have another free day play with the two recovered kickballs. The third one was currently orbiting in Mr. Hambrick's class. Funny enough, he trimmed his beard and Queeneka didn't even have to tell him.

Keely's parents sent boxes full of The Scoop Troop shirts to school for the students. Queeneka felt embarrassed wearing it to school at first, but it made people laugh. Veronica wore the shirt next and it soon became a trend. Even that big fourth grader wore one of The Scoop Troop shirts to school. Keely said that their family business was taking off.

Keely never did wear that stained peach-polka-dotted sweatshirt to school again. She came over to Queeneka's house but she didn't borrow a sweater, or anything else for that matter. They did have fun talking, though. Queeneka and Keely were eager to solve a new case together. Maybe Queeneka could find a job in fashion AND as a detective someday.

How to Solve a Mystery, by Queeneka

I love fashion just as much as I love a good mystery. When those kickballs went missing, I really wanted to solve the case. To get started, I spent time searching for the kickballs during PE class, just to make sure they hadn't been misplaced.

To dig in deeper, I checked out the box they were delivered in. To solve a mystery, you have to examine every possible connection. The box was empty, but I did find a piece of paper with a blurry logo on it. Then I went straight to the person closest to the case: Keely. Since her parents donated the balls, I thought she might have some important information. I hit a dead end when she didn't give me much information.

Next, I thought about the other people who might have seen the balls before they disappeared. To solve a mystery, it's important to ask a lot of questions. I talked to the custodian to see if he knew about the box or the kickballs. Score! He helped me figure out when the kickballs were removed from the box.

Good detectives keep their eyes open for anything suspicious. When I noticed the sun in Mr. Hambrick's solar system model looked like a red ball, I questioned him about it. The answers weren't clear and he sure seemed guilty! I followed this up by talking to Mr. Sleuth for more answers. Keely was on my case the whole time.

Keeping an eye out for details helped me solve the case. My big breakthrough came when I saw a group of fourth graders playing with a kickball. What I found out from them led me to the answers!

Q & A with Keely

If you had to do it all again, what would you do differently?
My parents were nice enough to send the kickballs and I should've just accepted things sooner. Hiding the kickballs wasn't the right thing to do and I would've been more honest. I wouldn't want to change the outcome at all, though. The outcome was pretty great.

What was the worst part of the case for you?
I didn't want anyone to find out that I hid the kickballs! It was bad enough my parents started a weird new business and I had to wear a shirt with their logo on it. Queeneka just wouldn't give up! I worried what would happen if everyone saw the logo and then what would happen if they found out what I'd done.

How are things going for you now?
The business has really grown and my parents are happy about that. While I was embarrassed at first, I think it is cool that they're helping keep backyards clean and

stuff. Plus, they're able to spend a lot of time with me and my allowance has gone up. I didn't think the shirts would've become a trend—I really thought I was going to get teased all of the time! Best of all, Queeneka and I are good friends now.

If you were going to start your own business someday, what would it be?
Queeneka and I talked about this and we'd like to be detectives someday. That would be awesome if we had our own detective shop! Queeneka wants to combine this with fashion, but I'm not so sure about that.

Discussion Questions

1. Would you be embarrassed to wear The Scoop Troop shirt? Why or why not?

2. Has any member of your family embarrassed you at school? Was it more or less embarrassing than Keely's kickballs?

3. If you were in Keely's position, would you hide the kickballs? Why or why not?

4. Who did you suspect was guilty and why?

5. Do you think Mr. Hambrick had a reason to feel guilty using the kickball in his solar system?

Vocabulary

Here is a list of some important words in the story. Use the words in a sentence or create flashcards for practice. Try to create a song using at least five of the vocabulary words.

bouquet: a bunch of flowers

budget: amount to spend

courtyard: closed in area outside

dwarf planet: like a small planet but not quite

explanation: make something clear

fluorescent: extremely bright in color

hedges: a fence made out of shrubs

interrogation: questioning

logo: symbol for products

lumberjack: a person who cuts trees

lunged: a sudden reach

sidetracked: distracted

tampering: interfering

vanish: disappear

volunteers: helpers

Writing Prompt

Write a mystery featuring a character who solves a case about a missing jump rope. What happened to the jump rope and how did your character figure things out?

Write about a mystery in your life. What happened and how was the mystery solved?

Websites to Visit

Outdoor games you can play:
http://pbskids.org/zoom/activities/games

Learn more about the solar system:
https://solarsystem.nasa.gov/kids

Learn more about kickball and variations of the game:
http://familyfitness.about.com/od/Games-And-How-To-Play-Them/a/Kickball-Games-And-Variations.htm

About the Author

J. L. Anderson solves a mystery of her own almost every day like figuring out why her daughter is suddenly so quiet (what did she get into this time?), which of her two dogs stole the bag of treats, 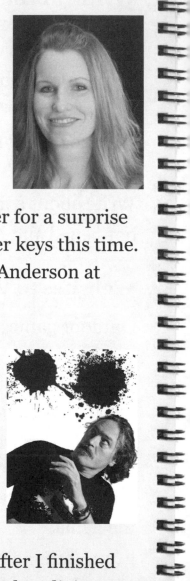 where her husband is taking her for a surprise dinner, or what happened to her keys this time. You can learn more about J.L. Anderson at www.jessicaleeanderson.com.

About the Illustrator

I have always loved drawing from a very young age. While I was at school, most of my time was spent drawing comics and copying my favorite characters.  With a portfolio under my arm, I started drawing comics for newspapers and fanzines. After I finished my studies I decided to try to make a living as a freelance illustrator... and here I am!